BALLOON

For Judy and Larry

First published in hardback in Great Britain by HarperCollins Publishers Ltd in 1998.
First published in Picture Lions in 1999.

1 3 5 7 9 10 8 6 4 2
ISBN 0 00 664 624–7

Picture Lions is an imprint of the Children's Division, part of HarperCollins Publishers Ltd,
77–85 Fulham Palace Road, Hammersmith, London W6 8JB.

Printed and bound in Singapore by Imago.

BALLOON

Jez Alborough

PictureLions

An Imprint of HarperCollinsPublishers

Billy saw it

Mummy bought it

Man threw it

Billy caught it.

Billy pulled it and waved it

Billy headed   and saved it.

Billy squeezed it   Billy tossed it

Billy missed it and lost it.

Mummy saw it   Mummy chased it

Dog barked   Dog raced it.

Dog jumped   Dog whacked it

Duck quacked...

and attacked it.

Cow licked it

Cow flicked it

Cow mooed and Cow kicked it. Bird flipped it

and flapped it   Tree tangled   and trapped it.

Wind threw it   Wind caught it

Wind blew it   and...

...brought it.

Billy chased it   Billy...

...stopped it.

But tripped up

and...

popped it.

Mummy sighed, Dog looked glum, Billy saw...

another one!